BERNAL & FLORINDA

A Spanish Tale

BY ERIC A. KIMMEL
ILLUSTRATED BY ROBERT RAYEVSKY

Holiday House / New York

Library of Congress Cataloging-in-Publication Data
Kimmel, Eric A.
Bernal and Florinda : a Spanish tale / by Eric A. Kimmel ;
illustrated by Robert Rayevsky. — 1st ed.
p.   cm.
Summary: A clever but poor cavalier wins the hand of his
true love by outwitting her father, the wealthy mayor of Seville.
ISBN 0-8234-1089-7
[1. Fairy tales.   2. Spain—Fiction.]   I. Rayevsky, Robert, ill.
II. Title.
PZ8.K527Bg   1994   93-37917   CIP   AC
[E]—dc20

For Carol and Barry
E.A.K.

To Claire
R.R.

Author's Note

Bernal & Florinda is an original story written in the tradition of the Spanish picaresque tale. The idea for the story began one summer when my wife, Doris, and I were driving along Hurricane Ridge in Olympic National Park. Every square inch of the road was covered with grasshoppers. Doris, who hates grasshoppers, said, "God must like these things. Why else would He make so many of them?" Even so, she wouldn't get out of the car.

—E.A.K.

Artist's Note

The tale of *Bernal & Florinda* reminded me of early European theatrical productions. That inspired me to draw the characters like actors, in a stylized and exaggerated way, using pen and ink and "brilliant" watercolors. I drew the bright, colorful Spanish landscapes in the background as if they were stage decorations.

—R.R.

Once upon a time two young lovers lived in the city of Seville. Their names were Bernal and Florinda. Bernal was a dashing cavalier who possessed considerable charm and wit, but hardly any wealth to speak of. His sole property was an overgrown field swarming with grasshoppers. Florinda, on the other hand, was the daughter of Don Garcilaso, the town's mayor and one of the richest men in Spain. He cared nothing for love. Only money.

Every evening Bernal would steal beneath Florinda's balcony and serenade her with his guitar.

"Ay, Florinda, sweet flower of love,
Your dark eyes set my soul aflame."

And Florinda, blushing behind her fan, would throw down a red rose.

One night, instead of a rose, Bernal received a bucket of cold water.

"Be gone, you vagabond!" Don Garcilaso shouted from the balcony. "I forbid you to speak to my daughter ever again!"

Though drenched to the skin, Bernal bowed politely. "*Señor Alcalde*, do not despise me because I am poor. I love Florinda and wish to marry her. With your permission, of course."

Don Garcilaso replied with scorn, "Impudent rascal! What will you live on? Grasshoppers from your field, I suppose?" Then he added, "I would rather see Florinda marry the son of a wandering tinker. He could at least support her by mending pots and pans."

This was a grave insult, one that called for a duel with swords or pistols. Bernal did not own a pistol, and his sword was a rusty relic left to him by his grandfather. Nonetheless, he answered with the pride of his ancestors, who were all knights and gentlemen. "Don Garcilaso, as much as you insult me, you cannot erase what is written in my heart. I love Florinda. I will marry her in spite of you. And I will make my fortune from those grasshoppers."

Bold words. But words are one thing, deeds another. Dawn found Bernal standing in his field while the grasshoppers swarmed around him.

"These creatures must be good for something. Why else would the Good Lord make so many?" Bernal set out to discover the Good Lord's purpose. He spent the morning catching grasshoppers until he filled a sackful. Then he started down the road with the bulging sack of clicking, buzzing insects slung over his shoulder.

Along the way he met a goose boy driving a flock of honking, hissing geese to market.

"What noisy creatures!" Bernal remarked.

"Poor things. They are hungry, and I have no food for them," the goose boy replied.

"Geese like grasshoppers. Here is a whole sackful. What will you give me for it?" Bernal asked.

The goose boy's face brightened. "Take one of my geese."

Bernal poured out the grasshoppers in front of the geese, who devoured them all. Selecting a fine goose, he stuffed it in the sack and continued on his way.

By and by he passed a forge. The blacksmith stood by the door, sighing.

"Why so sad?" Bernal asked.

"Ay, ay, ay!" moaned the blacksmith. "My daughter is to be married tomorrow. I was supposed to buy a goose for the wedding feast, but I forgot. Now my wife is going to kill me!"

"I have a goose," Bernal said. "What will you give me for it?"

"A sack full of charcoal."

Bernal traded the goose for charcoal. Slinging the heavy sack over his shoulder, he trudged along.

Farther on, Bernal passed by a candlemaker's shop. Hearing screams from inside, he looked through the door. He saw the candlemaker chasing his apprentice around the shop with a stick.

"Don't hit that boy," Bernal said.

"He deserves what he gets, and more," the candlemaker replied. "I told him to order more charcoal, but he forgot, and now we have run out of fuel. The fire is out, the wax is hardening, and a whole day's labor is lost."

"Is it charcoal you need? Here is a sackful. What will you give me for it?"

"As many candles as you can carry." Bernal emptied out the charcoal, then filled his sack with fine white candles. With the sackful of candles slung over his shoulder, he started down the road once more.

After a while he came to an inn. A rascally-looking innkeeper stood in the doorway. He wore a black cloak and a three-cornered hat. An eyepatch covered his left eye. He was beating his breast and wailing, "I am lost. Woe is me!"

"What happened?" Bernal asked.

"Behold the troubles that pursue me," the innkeeper groaned. He opened the inn door.

Bernal saw a dead man, a wandering tinker, lying on the floor. Pots and pans lay scattered around him.

"I will summon the authorities," said Bernal.

The innkeeper turned pale. "Don't do that! I am in enough trouble with them already. If they come here and find this man dead, they will accuse me of murder. I swear it is not my fault. The tinker came to my inn and asked for fruit. I gave him peaches. Is it my fault the greedy guts tried to swallow them whole? A peach pit lodged in his throat. The next moment he was stretched out on the floor, dead as a stone. Woe is me! What will I do?"

"I can help you," said Bernal. "Take the candles that are in my sack to the nearest church. Light them so that the poor tinker's soul may find its way to heaven. Meanwhile, I will carry his body to Seville. Don Garcilaso, the mayor, is a friend of mine. I will explain the situation to him. He will arrange for a discreet but honorable funeral."

The innkeeper kissed Bernal's hand. "Señor, may the Good Lord drop a thousand blessings on your head if you perform this kindness for me."

Bernal emptied the candles from the sack. Then he stuffed the tinker inside with all his pots and pans. Borrowing the innkeeper's cloak, hat, and eyepatch, Bernal started down the road to Seville.

He arrived at the siesta hour. Not a soul was about. Bernal hurried through the deserted streets until he reached Don Garcilaso's house. Swiftly he emptied out his sack. He propped the tinker against the wall and arranged the pots in front of him. Then he went around the corner to wait.

In a while the door opened. Don Garcilaso came out. He glanced at the tinker, then at the pots. He picked up the smallest one.

"How much is this pot?"

The tinker, of course, said nothing. Don Garcilaso spoke louder.

"I said, 'How much is this pot!'"

No answer. Don Garcilaso grew angry.

"What is the matter with you? Are you asleep?"

Still no reply. Don Garcilaso lost his temper. "You will answer when the mayor speaks to you!" He gave the tinker a box on the ear. The tinker toppled over. At that moment Bernal came rushing around the corner.

"Murder! The mayor has killed my father!"

His hue and cry brought the whole town running.

"What has happened?"

"The mayor has killed an innocent man, a poor tinker."

"That rascally skinflint has gone too far. Does he think his wealth gives him the right to murder honest citizens?"

"Villain! He will pay for this! To the gallows with him!"

"The gallows! The gallows!" cried the people of Seville.

Don Garcilaso threw himself on his knees before Bernal. (He did not recognize him because of his disguise.) "Mercy, *Señor!* I did not mean to hurt your father. It was an accident. I swear!"

Bernal frowned. "Even if that were true, it makes no difference. I am a poor man. My father is dead. How am I to bury him?"

"I will build a marble tomb for your father. I will bury him as if he were my own. Only tell these people I am innocent!"

"That is all very well for my father, but what about me?" Bernal replied. "How will I earn my living? Who will help me mend the pots now that my father is dead?"

"I am a wealthy man," Don Garcilaso pleaded. "I will give you a house and lands. You will never have to mend pots again."

"Wealth feeds the body, not the soul," Bernal replied, wiping a tear from his eye. "My father was my closest friend. Now I must live alone."

"Not so!" said Don Garcilaso. "I have a daughter, Florinda. She is beautiful and charming. Marry her. She will make a fine companion. Only tell these people I am innocent!"

Bernal gasped. "You are jesting. Am I to believe that the noble Don Garcilaso, the mayor of Seville, one of the wealthiest men in Spain, would offer his daughter to the son of a wandering tinker?"

"It is true! Believe me!"

"Then I accept," said Bernal. "On one condition. That Florinda wishes to marry me." He lifted the eyepatch, flung off the cloak, and doffed the innkeeper's three-cornered hat.

"I've been tricked!" Don Garcilaso screamed when he recognized Bernal.

But not before Florinda, looking down from the balcony, cried out, "I do!"

Don Garcilaso was furious, but he had to fulfill his promises just the same. The good people of Seville saw to that. Bernal and Florinda were married in the cathedral, with Don Garcilaso's reluctant, but no less valid, blessing. Thus in the end Bernal kept his vow. He married Florinda in spite of her father, and he did make his fortune from those grasshoppers.

And what of the tinker? He was laid to rest in a splendid tomb. Or more correctly, he was almost laid to rest. For as the pall-bearers carried the coffin into the crypt, one stumbled, jarring the peach pit loose from the tinker's throat.

The tinker came back to life. He opened his eyes, pushed open the coffin lid, and sat up.

"That rascally innkeeper!" he cried in horror. "I meant to spend one night, not eternity!" He leaped from the coffin and ran from the crypt as fast as his legs could carry him.

He never appeared in those parts again. But to this day a splendid marble tomb stands in the cathedral of Seville. Visitors often ask what duke or prince is buried there. The truth is, it was intended for a wandering tinker, but not even he is there now.

The only thing inside is a peach pit.